Little Red Riding Hood

Retold by Lyn Calder
Illustrated by Terri Super

MERRIGOLD PRESS • NEW YORK

Golden Books Publishing Company Inc., New York, New York 10106

Once upon a time there lived a little girl
who had a beautiful red cloak with a hood.
The little girl wore it every day, and that is
why she was called Little Red Riding Hood.

One day Little Red Riding Hood's mother said, "Your grandmother is not feeling well. I want you to take these honey cakes to her. Now, remember, do not stop to speak with anyone and do not leave the path."

"I will remember!" said Little Red Riding Hood.

Little Red Riding Hood set out for Grandmother's house. Soon a wolf came along and spoke to her. "Where are you off to so early?" the wolf asked.

And Little Red Riding Hood forgot what her mother had told her and answered, "I'm taking these honey cakes to my grandmother. She is not feeling well."

"I'm sorry to hear that," said the wolf.

But the wolf was really not sorry at all.

"Where does your grandmother live?" asked the wolf.

"Grandmother lives in the cottage past the windmill," said Little Red Riding Hood.

"I see," said the wolf. "Why don't you pick a bouquet for your grandmother?" he suggested, pointing to some wildflowers.

"I'm not supposed to leave the path," answered Little Red Riding Hood. "But I am sure Grandmother would like such pretty flowers!" So Little Red Riding Hood left the path to pick some.

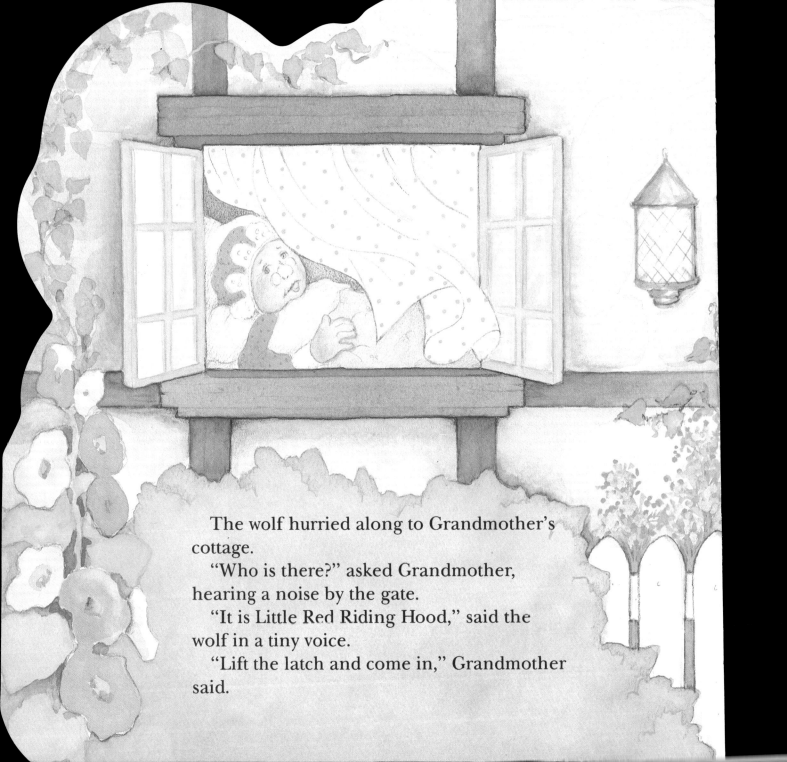

The wolf hurried along to Grandmother's cottage.

"Who is there?" asked Grandmother, hearing a noise by the gate.

"It is Little Red Riding Hood," said the wolf in a tiny voice.

"Lift the latch and come in," Grandmother said.

The wolf went in and ate up Grandmother—one—two—three!

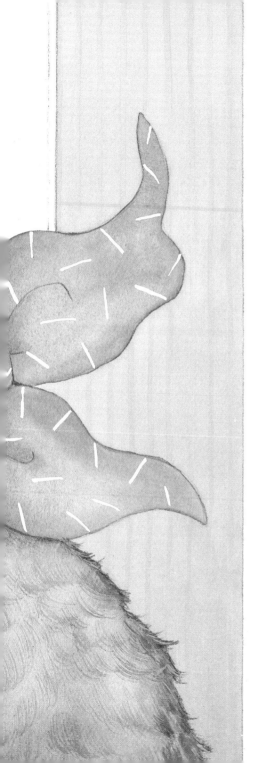

Then he put on Grandmother's
nightgown and nightcap and
climbed into her bed.

When Little Red Riding Hood reached
Grandmother's cottage, she was surprised to
find the gate open. And when she walked in,
she knew something was not right.

"Grandmother, what big ears you have!" said Little Red Riding Hood.

"The better to hear you with, my dear."

"What big eyes you have!" said Little Red Riding Hood.

"The better to see you with, my dear."

"What big teeth you have!" said Little Red Riding Hood.

"The better to eat you with, my dear!"

Then the wolf jumped out of bed and ate up Little Red Riding Hood—one—two—three!

All at once the wolf grew sleepy and climbed back into bed for a nap. He was snoring loudly when a hunter passed the cottage and heard him.

The hunter went inside and saw the wolf. "I've got you at last, you wicked wolf!" the hunter said. And he killed the wolf—one—two—three!

The hunter saw that the wolf looked very fat. So he carefully cut the wolf open.

Snip, snip. Out popped Little Red Riding Hood.

Snip, snip. Out popped Grandmother. They hugged each other tightly.

After dragging the wolf outside, the hunter sat down with Grandmother and Little Red Riding Hood, and the three of them feasted on the honey cakes.

Soon Grandmother was feeling better. "We won't ever have to worry about the wicked wolf again," she said.

Little Red Riding Hood set out for home.
As she hurried along she said, over and over,
"I won't ever leave the path again when
Mother tells me not to. I promise!"
   She never did, and she lived happily ever
after.